Trumpicana

Presley Acuna

Kendall Smith

© 2016

PERCUSSION
PUBLISHING

Percussion Publishing LLC
New York, NY

For information about bulk purchases, contact Percussion Publishing Bulk Sales:
PercPubOrders@percussionpublishing.com

Percussion Publishing can bring authors to your live event. For more information or to book an event, write to: Authors@PercussionPublishing.com. For all other inquiries, contact: Administration@percussionpublishing.com

Visit us online to find out news about present and future publishing projects:

www.PercussionPublishing.com

To all American voters.   Use it or lose it.

Authors' Prefaces

The stories contained herein are satirical in nature. As such they have a purpose. And it is not always to make you laugh. But it is always to make you think.

Satire walks a line. It uses wit for the purpose of social criticism by treating the ridiculous as normal. That is our goal, in writing these stories for your amusement. We want to make you think, and keep thinking long after you put down these stories, about the current state of American politics.

The current election cycle has been called many things: a circus, a travesty, a grass roots revolution, an uprising of the disenfranchised middle class, but what is most fascinating about it is the way abnormal is immediately subsumed into the cultural consciousness and becomes normal almost as soon as it occurs. Inch by inch, sound bite by sound bite, we have been led from the sublime to the ridiculous, and it is now the new sublime.

You could make the argument that the current Presidential election process is, in and of itself, a satire of elections past, back when our heads fit more sturdily on the threads of our necks, and there were filters for the insanity that prevails today. Truth is stranger than fiction.

But as writers, fiction is our weapon of choice. And it is a potent weapon. While these stories might be classified as satires, they are also meant to scare you. These things could happen. With these stories you are about to read, we hope to galvanize you into action, into activism, into the voting booth. Don't let our stories come true!

- Presley Acuna

If there's one thing to take solace in during this unusual election process, it is the rights our forefathers handed down to us. It is our duty to uphold these values, to cherish and respect them and enjoy the freedoms they provide. It is not the time to hunker down in fear, to shun political engagement or to consternate on what could or could not happen.

It is time to take a stand and participate, no matter what your point of view may be or your beliefs. It is critical your voice is heard, even if it is simply amongst friends who share similar concerns. Doing nothing and being apathetic to the process presents the greater risk.

That risk... of remaining stagnant, in a time of swirling anger and potential upheaval and choosing not to have a voice... that risks the very rights granted to us by the constitution. Many who think they are insulated or above the fray may find themselves in the near future challenged with a revised set of national ideals that have no connection to their goals or ambitions.

The publication of this novella represents our response to the situation at hand. Satire, the use of humor, prognosticating into the future about where our Democracy could go in the years to follow: if we help to illuminate just how far we've veered away from a normal election cycle, then we can say we accomplished something.

Our choice is to use satirical short stories to express our concerns, a freedom provided by the first amendment. We hope you find our stories entertaining, but more importantly...

... We hope you find the courage to engage and elect leaders that will take us to a higher plateau.

- Kendall Smith

In America, anyone can become president.
That's the problem. -George Carlin

TRUMPICANA: CONTENTS

White House Arrest

By Kendall Smith

"So help me God."

A roar of voices and applause rose from the crowd when the man removed his right hand from the bible. The sound grew louder. For a brief moment, she could have sworn the Chief Justice of the United States hesitated before shaking the new President's hand.

Courtney Harper looked out to see a hundred thousand people, most of whom were older white men, holler and jump with excitement. They got their man, she said to herself.

In her earpiece, she heard her top lieutenant say, "Man in black, right of stage."

"Got em. Roof check one?"

"Copy that. Spotted. Clear lines, over."

The Director of the Secret Service glanced towards the right side of the stage but did not concern herself with the exchange. She knew the men speaking in her intercom intimately as she had worked alongside them for over twenty-five years. There was no angle, nor any line of sight

1

that was unaccounted for. A dozen snipers on roofs held the high ground while a hundred plain-clothed agents wove through the crowds. Two dozen elite agents from the Presidential Protective Division flanked the inauguration stage.

If the suspicious man in black so much as winced, the crosshairs aimed at his skull would re-calibrate for the motion. Her department's personnel were operating in fifth gear and ready to pounce on the slightest physical threat to the new President, Ronald Drumpf.

The protestors in the distance, cordoned off from those in support of the new POTUS, had several hundred police officers to keep them in check. There were contingency plans if those protesters broke through the steel-rod street gates. President Drumpf would be informed he had several minutes to conclude his speech before the risk of a full-on riot broke out on the great lawn in front of the U.S. Capitol.

Courtney watched President Drumpf grab the sides of the podium and grin from ear to ear. When he raised his hands, the crowd followed suit: a gesture and reciprocation that had become all too familiar in the general election. The crowd joined voices to chant, "Drumpf! Drumpf! Woot, woot, woot!"

"I cannot believe we did it! I'm so honored."

She listened to him speak, and in true form, the pronoun, 'I,' was used in almost every sentence.

He went on ad nauseam about his greatness, but unlike his 44 predecessors, he made the event solely about himself.

She ground her teeth while listening, and based on the interviews she'd seen on the news the evening prior, many felt the same way. If you were a woman, a black man, gay or an immigrant, it was hard not to feel mentally violated by the man on stage.

The sentiments of those who opposed the new President had intensified in the months preceding the November election. As divisive as Drumpf's rhetoric was, the tenor of the election turned three shades darker one week before the final vote. The candidate had unleashed a devastating attack on his opponent's character, which further divided the electorate and changed the electoral map in his favor. Florida and Ohio caved, which resulted in the narrowest victory ever recorded in a presidential election.

Courtney knew she had to remain unbiased. Her stellar twenty-plus years of service had carried her to the top position in the Secret Service. She would personally report to the new President, whom she would meet for the first time seven hours from now.

However, it was not the first time Drumpf had made an impact on her life. She watched President Drumpf's hair flop in the wind like a small animal drunk on fermented berries. She recalled the first time Drumpf threw her parents' lives into chaos.

April 1, 1989, Miami Florida

Courtney toweled herself off in the bathroom and

3

dressed before entering the living room. She heard her parents speaking in hushed tones. Her older brother, a junior in college, was staring out the window. She turned to see her usually optimistic father looking glum, if not outright desperate. Sitting on the couch, his shoulders slumped forward as he rubbed his temples.

He didn't look at her when he said, "He screwed us." His head sank on his chest.

"Who did?" Courtney's eyes tracked back and forth from one relative to another.

"Drumpf." Her brother shook his head.

She watched as her father turned to make eye contact with her. "While you were at the beach. We met with him. He's not going to pull the trigger on the development."

Her heart stuttered. "Abuela Vista?"

Her brother raised his arms before he said, "Obviously," and then dropped them in disgust.

Her father sighed while her mother rubbed his back. Courtney had never seen him so unsettled. A former New York police lieutenant, he'd put every penny of his savings into a land deal several years' prior in the hope of flipping it to a development company. It was obvious negotiations had not gone her father's way.

"He was right there, in the background the whole time, just waiting to pounce."

Courtney took a seat. "Ronald Drumpf was there?"

"Your father did everything he could," her mother said.

"Eileen, stop." Her father rose to his feet and staggered towards the window. "At the end of the negotiation, he just said… dump it. My partners were just as shocked as I was.' For a moment, he seemed ready to cry, which she had seldom witnessed. "There's no reasoning with him, we even offered to lower the price of the land."

"Just say it dad, he's an asshole," said her brother.

"Well, another company might bite."

"After Drumpf ran up the bidding? And drove all the other players out of the deal? Not likely, not in this market."

"I should have pressed him."

"That's the understatement of the year."

Her mother rose from the couch. "Zip it. Your father's been through enough."

Courtney's heart sunk as the three exchanged verbal jabs. Her father's dream of parlaying a one hundred-thousand-dollar investment into a comfortable retirement was off the table. Her thoughts turned to her own circumstances.

"What does that mean for us?"

"We'll get by dear, don't fret."

Her brother stepped forward. "You're going to need student loans. I have to do the same for my senior year."

"Jesus." She did the math in her head and wondered how, without her parent's support, she could ever pay off a four-year college loan. "Is this really happening?"

Her father turned to her. It took him a moment to make eye contact with her. "I am so sorry, Courtney."

Her mother moved closer. "It's not your father's fault." She then turned and made sure her son saw her expression.

Exacerbated, he complied to his mother's glare by saying, "Drumpf stabbed us in the back."

Inauguration Day, 2017

Her earpiece sounded off again when another possible threat was identified. Her subordinates were on top of matters, which did not surprise her. As the memories of her family's experience mixed with the sound of Drumpf's self-aggrandizing oration, she found herself grinning.

The man behind the podium had no clue how a nineteen eighties business decision had almost ruined her family's small nest egg. He'd find out soon enough, and if everything went according to plan, the country would be better off because of it.

Operation Abuela Vista was about to unfold, her departments code name and one of her choosing. She wasn't alone. A host of Washington DC power brokers had her back and she could claim she was simply following orders.

10:15 p.m., The White House

"Excellent, I must say, excellent." Drumpf clasped his hands behind his back and sauntered around the Oval Office. She watched him tilt his chin up and look through the bullet-proof windows that framed a view of the Washington Monument in the distance.

"You know, that monument could use a little flair." He chuckled.

Courtney surveyed the room full of Drumpf's top advisors and noted how much they were savoring their moment of glory.

Someone from the back of the room said, "It's time for your picture at the desk, President Drumpf."

"Ah, yes. Should I roll up my sleeves, like Obama did?" No one in the crowd responded. "Nah!" President Drumpf waved his hands in jest and a chorus of laughter followed.

She watched him casually walk around to the seat of Presidential power. The sound of pressed leather filled the room as the cushion adjusted to the ass pressing down on it. He swiveled for a moment, back and forth while a smirk appeared on his face and then vanished. The photographer wove through the crowd and pointed his lens at the man, who responded by clasping his hands and grinning. A moment later, he replaced the grin and provided a scowl, one that reminded her of the look he often provided on a reality TV show.

"Let's try this side." He turned his head and the camera followed. After several takes, the new President said. "Have we got a good one?"

The photographer stepped back. "Absolutely. I'll need some time—."

"Let's see em'." Drumpf waved him closer to the desk. After trying to position himself to show the LCD screen to the President, Drumpf simply took the camera out of his hands.

"Johnny, Fred, come here."

Courtney scanned the crowd and watched several people exchange awkward glances.

The two advisors moved around the desk and leaned over the screen. Drumpf hit a button. "That one's pretty good."

"The next one sir, that's it."

"Nah," Drumpf shook his head, "my bad side. But look at *that* one."

The three of them said 'ah' in unison and then pushed buttons to go back and forth between two pictures.

"The light's not good there," said Fred while the Press Secretary nodded.

"Obviously. What am I paying you guys for?" Drumpf shook his head, tapped a button and followed with, "That's it. That's the one. It looks great, don't ya think?"

The two nodded and high fived one another while Drumpf's smiled and handed the camera back to the photographer.

"I want that pic sent out immediately to every news outlet."

"Yes sir."

His Chief of Staff provided a mocking salute. "Good idea."

Drumpf looked at him. "Should we take some more pictures of me tomorrow?"

"We've got a full agenda, I'm afraid."

"Oh, yeah... well everyone knows I love a good photo op."

"We can use that to our advantage. More visuals…" the Press Secretary began to nod and looked at Drumpf, "that will help us own the media, like you have for the past nine months!"

A chorus of laughter rose but Courtney remained stone faced.

As Drumpf shook hands and bid farewell to his colleagues and cronies, the crowd filtered out until only four remained: Drumpf's Chief of Staff, Courtney, and two other secret service agents.

She painted a smile for the man in charge. "Congratulations again, President Drumpf."

"Thank you, Courtney. That will be all."

"Not quite," her eyes turned to the Chief of Staff, "Would you excuse us, please?"

The chief snorted but she cut him off before he could speak. "Security protocols, sir. We need to assure the President knows how we will manage the next few days, if not years."

He chuckled at that. "Okay there, dear."

Courtney took the condescending tone in stride. She knew she could knock out the portly man with one punch.

"Well, Mr. President, we'll kick things off tomorrow morning then?"

"Eight sharp."

"As you wish." The man took his leave.

Courtney glanced at her agents and with a quick tilt of the head, they were gone. She remained alone with the President. "I will keep this brief, as we have an hour on the

9

schedule tomorrow morning."

"Might have to dial that back to thirty. Let's get this over with."

"Of course, your family is upstairs, waiting for you."

"Uh huh." He nodded.

"Bear in mind that any time you are anywhere inside or outside the White House you will be accompanied by a security detail. There are no exceptions, outside of official meetings and your private residence on the second floor. Even upstairs, agents will be in present in the main hallway. For security's sake."

He yawned and she could see the dental work in the back of his mouth. Classless, she thought.

"And in terms of communication. We've collected your family's mobile devices. I need yours as well."

"Come again?"

"Your cell phone. Do you have more than one?"

"Yes." She held out her hands and grinned. "Welcome to the Presidency. We need to debug your phone and provide secure lines of communication."

He rolled his eyes, stood up and reached down in his pants pocket. He fumbled and took his time. She wondered why it was taking so long. Was the dick having trouble distinguishing his manhood from the tool in question, or was the tool in question having an issue distinguishing his phone from his dick?

He handed over two mobile phones. "Thank you, sir. Gerald outside the main door will take you to the First Lady."

"Very well."

The two left the room and entered the main hallway. She watched President Drumpf saunter around the corner with an agent in tow.

When he did so, she walked towards another room and found her gear bag. Within it, she retrieved her intercom, a Glock nine millimeter and holster, and two cans of Red Bull. Courtney cracked open one can and chugged it. She tossed it in a waste bin and waited patiently for Gerald, her number two, to return downstairs.

He arrived in five minutes' time and walked up to her. "POTUS is tending to his wife. He decided to use the Lincoln bedroom."

"Not the Presidential suite?"

"Nope. He said he wanted to break in every bed, starting with the most famous."

"Figures. Okay," she exhaled, "you ready?" She handed him a can of Red Bull.

"Everyone is."

She turned on the intercom and in a commanding voice, said, "Operation Abuela Vista is a go. Commence."

***

Harold, the civilian security guard at the gate, waved goodbye to the Chief of Staff as he passed him. The security officer closed the sliding glass window to keep the confines of his guard booth warm. He then turned to press the button to close the iron gates to the White House. It did not respond. "What the…" He hit it again and rubbed his chin. A moment later, he saw what appeared to be dozens of black vans approaching the entrance.

He slammed his finger on the red button but nothing happened. "Son of a bitch!" He grabbed the phone to alert higher authorities. "Checkpoint one here, gates are not closing, I need—."

"That will be all, Harold."

His head swiveled to see Courtney Harper standing outside the glass window. She opened it.

"But Director Harper, the vans!"

"That's our detail. You're excused for the evening. We'll take it from here." She waved the vans onto the grounds and they streamed by in what appeared to be an unending tide of black vehicles.

"This is not protocol, I need to alert—!"

"No, you don't, we're the Secret Service, you are not." She snatched the intercom out of his hand. "We'll let you know when we're ready for you to return to work. Leave the grounds. Now."

Courtney turned and saw dozens of men exiting the vehicles. She whistled and caught their attention. "Wait for my order!" she yelled.

One of her agents escorted Harold to the employee parking area to ensure he left the White House grounds. The same agent reappeared a minute later.

She moved towards the entrance, opened the door and found a half a dozen agents and twenty others who represented the White House civilian night shift. As ordered, they had gathered in the East Room. She came to a stop in the middle of what appeared to be a very concerned audience. "Ladies and Gentlemen, thanks for coming."

"We didn't have a choice," complained one of the cooks.

"Exactly. Some of you I know, some I do not. We appreciate your services, however we are asking all of you to leave the White House grounds and return only when asked to do so." She placed her hands on her hips and waited for the news to settle in with the staff.

"Excuse me, what are telling us?"

"Your counterparts on the day shift are being given the same notice." As the men and women started to eye each other, she added quickly, "Your salary and benefits will continue."

"Come again? You can't—."

"The Secret Service is taking over. With that said, you're excused, please leave immediately." The crowd fired off more questions while the security agents began escorting them out of the building. It took all of sixty seconds to clear the White House of anyone who was not a member of Drumpf's immediate family or members of the Secret Service.

She moved to the main entrance and waited patiently by the door. When her intercom confirmed the night shift's departure, she replied and said, "Move in people, let's go."

She stepped away and both doors opened wide. A rush of manpower stormed toward her. She nodded to some, others she directed to particular rooms and offices. Two men carried a large black trunk that appeared to contain something extremely heavy. They went straight to the basement. People poured through the doors, and she imagined what it looked like from outside the White House: a torrent of black-clad men and women sweeping through the entrance like a S.W.A.T. team.

Black vans continued to drive up, unload, and depart. In sheer numbers, the group represented an unprecedented assembly of security personnel, the likes of which had never been gathered in the history of the service. They sprawled out in various directions, with one exception: the soundproof rooms on the second floor were off limits. Every man and woman entering the White House was there on her orders and executing a plan Congressional leaders believed was best for the country.

With that thought in mind, she retrieved her cell phone and placed the only call she would make that evening. It would be, until a time of her choosing, the last call made from the executive branch of government.

On the third ring, the Speaker of the House answered. "Yes?"

"Operation Abuela Vista has commenced. Do I have your authority to move forward, Speaker Bryan?"

"Please do so. Your country thanks you."

"Excellent. Your representative will be here at 7:30 a.m.?"

"He'll be there."

"Very well then, I'll call you after we inform POTUS in the morning."

"Please do."

She ended the call and saw five men towing what appeared to be welding equipment. "The Oval Office, start there."

"Yes ma'am."

**

Seven men entered the Oval Office and turned on the lights. "Everything goes. You know what to do," said the officer in charge.

Two men walked around the desk. One ripped the phone line out of the socket while another confiscated the laptop. Drawers were checked but all were empty at present. Another man lifted a secret compartment in the floor and saw a mechanism that controlled recording equipment. He untethered them from the floor with a drill, grabbed the sides and yanked the recorder free from the wires connected to it. A woman removed a fake book in the cabinet and used a five-inch dagger to cut through wires attached to it. The invisible camera in the spine of the novel, a copy of Charles Dicken's *Great Expectations*, was rendered useless. Another man appeared rolling a large dump bin before him. The book was tossed in along with three phones, the laptop, and every device that could be used to record or communicate. One man entered and then left the bathroom a moment later with another phone. "Here's the phone from the executive crapper." It too was dumped in the garbage bin.

Courtney entered the room and started barking orders to double check for outlets that could provide communication with the outside world. A junior agent followed suit and took a hammer to several Ethernet connections.

The room reserved for the Chief of Staff underwent a similar disassembly while the windows were secured to insure no one could break through or open the bulletproof glass. The process took twenty minutes. The agents were enjoying themselves. One saw a black Wi-Fi router in the corner and smashed it with his boot before he kicked it across the wood floors. He laughed but his supervisor responded with a disappointing shake of the head. The team moved onto their next assignment.

A large pot hit the floor when a clumsy agent knocked it from a counter in the kitchen. The agents ignored the mess and moved straight to the windows. Three men assembled a blow torch. One of them placed a welding mask over his head. A moment later, he soldered the windows shut so they would never open. The only windows in the White House that could open and close were now sealed off to the outside world.

Twenty men stormed down the basement steps and entered the main communications center. A dozen went to work on the multitude of lines that enabled digital communication to and from the White House. With tools that looked like heavy-duty branch clippers, they went down the line and severed each and every phone, internet and video connection visible to the naked eye. Another man flung open steel doors that led to the servers that managed data and stored digital information. The room was a mix of heated and cooled air, the result of engineering that allowed for multiple servers to work in close proximity. The man walked over, pulled down a large lever that controlled the power, and suddenly a hundred blinking lights went dark. "The Internet's down, what a shame," the agent said. Four others entered and started yanking slim black boxes from their designated niches. They also had a large trash bin in tow, and all the servers piled up within it.

The press center was awash in debris, the result of removing all phone jacks, microphones, camera equipment and the podium itself. One agent caught the attention of Gerald who was inspecting the team's work. The second in command watched the junior agent point towards the hundred dangling wires above their heads. He responded by saying, "What's the issue? Clip em' all, now."

The Secret Service was well aware of the secret passages that led to and from the White House grounds. Several entry points were blocked off with an assembly of office equipment jammed between the walls, floor to ceiling. Hordes of men continued to collect and place furniture into nooks and crannies. Even if a person was able to clamber through the mess, he or she would find the blast-proof doors to the White House grounds bolted shut.

On the roof, ten men appeared and sprawled out in various directions. Antenna wiring was clipped while others used power drills to unfasten antenna dishes from the poles that held them. They started to collect in a pile near the entrance that led downstairs. Two snipers, roof team one, remained motionless as the others scurried about collecting anything that represented communication equipment.

When the agents finished they huddled around the pile of antenna dishes. Not knowing what to do next, they paused to enjoy the view of the Washington Monument on a cold night. "Beautiful isn't it?" said the tallest among them. The moment of Zen lingered, seeming to captivate them while the comment went unanswered.

Several minutes ticked by, and as men will do, they found ways to pass the time. One picked up a tiny stone, one of many littering the roof, and tossed it. Another followed suit and the man who tossed it aimed at one of the vans parked below. It took several tries, but soon enough the sound of a stone smacking on metal echoed from below. The man who had tossed the first stone laughed.

It escalated soon after that. One officer picked up a small 20-inch antenna dish. He noticed it only weighed several pounds. Upon further examination, he snapped off the projector extension. The other agents turned to watch the man examine the item he held. "Look, doesn't this look like a Frisbee?"

"Clever," said Edward, "what's your point?"

Chuck examined the item closely. "Makes one wonder... how far can it fly?"

The men shared looks, then laughter as they watched Chuck step towards to edge of the roof.

That evening, the first-ever White House antenna Frisbee competition took place. The first dish, and smallest, was lofted at 12:04 a.m. and flew into the night sky in an arc across the South Lawn. The moonlight illuminated its descent as it tipped to the right and silently crashed on the dormant grass.

"Damn, that was pretty good, Chuck!"

Inspired by Chuck's example, the others on the roof went to task and started breaking equipment and gathering up their own "Frisbees" so they could take part. One stepped forward, ten feet from the roofline, and whipped the antenna with all his might. A Frisbee expert, he was not, and it sliced vertically through the sky until it crashed and split into two near the White House.

The group hooted with laughter, but when they turned, the shortest agent among them held a three-foot wide dish in his hands. "Had to grab the biggest one, didn't you?"

"Tommy's got a Napoleonic complex, go figure." They chuckled until he stepped forward, holding the unwieldy object. "Wait, don't do it," said Chuck.

"Watch this," Tommy snarled at them over his shoulder, and then grabbed one side of the dish with both hands. He started to spin himself, to provide momentum like an Olympic hammer thrower. He looped around and around, faster and faster.

Edward raised his hands. "Stop!"

He released the massive dish, and it climbed in the sky to an unprecedented height, one that prompted future jokes about how Tommy had finally compensated for being so short. It rose to great lengths, and then, in a turn for the worse, the wind caught the spinning dish. It circled above, seeming to mock the man who tossed it, before it curved straight back to the White House. "Oh no," cried Tommy.

"It's going to hit the house!"

They all rushed to the edge and watched the speeding gray dish hit the side of a second-floor wall with a massive thud.

***

"Eek!" cried a young child in one of the bedrooms.

The two agents on guard exchanged looks. One agent spoke into his wrist intercom, "Anyone hear that?"

"Affirmative, what the hell was that?" said someone in his earpiece.

President Drumpf appeared in the hallway. He turned to see both agents staring at him. His comb over hair sat on his head like an electrocuted long-haired cat.

"Yes, Mr. President?"

"What in God's name was that?"

"What sir?"

"That loud bang!"

The man's granddaughter came running out of her room. "Grandpa!"

One agent stepped forward. "We didn't hear anything, sir."

Drumpf patted the small child's head. "It's okay sweetie." He turned to the agent, "Nothing, you say? Come on." He held his hands out and responded with his signature pout.

"Affirmative sir, we heard nothing," said the other agent.

President Drumpf escorted his granddaughter back to bed, and then reappeared. "I gotta tell you guys, I'm hearing a lot of weird sounds, is there something going on?"

The agent swallowed. If Drumpf made a move to go downstairs, he was authorized to confine him to his room. "Sir, this house is quite old, a lot of sounds echo through the walls." He shrugged his shoulders. "Probably the cleaning staff."

"And where are the phones? No phones in the private quarters?"

"Ah, being debugged, sir."

Drumpf shook his head, muttered "Unbelievable," and reentered the bedroom.

The agent stepped forward to look inside the room. He noticed the curtain was half open. He exhaled in relief, but a moment later in the window beyond, he noticed what appeared to be a gray flying saucer glide across the night sky. The President froze before his head moved in tandem with the arc of the saucer as it curved towards the earth. The agent watched to see what the President would do, and for a second he looked like he might turn and say something. He gave the agent a quizzical glance and then slammed the door shut.

There was no question an awkward moment had passed. The agent reminded himself just how awkward a moment it was for the entire country.

***

"Team roof two, is some dumbass up there tossing satellite dishes?"

Courtney put her hand on her hip and waited. She could visibly see one beyond on the South Lawn.

"Ah, yes, just having some fun, you know."

Courtney did her best to control her temper. She spoke into her comm and said, "Team roof one, do you copy?"

"Yes ma'am."

"Please advise team roof two that if they don't cut the bullshit, you have my authority to take them out."

Five seconds later, before one of the snipers spoke, she could clearly hear audible cries for mercy over the intercom. "You hearing this, chief?"

"Yup."

"On full automatic up here, given the size of the group. Waiting on your order, over."

She chuckled and decided to let the two teams work it out themselves.

She turned and saw twenty team members walking towards her. "West Wing is nearly finished."

She gestured with her hands towards one of the main hallways. "So... go to the East Wing." She pointed towards her watch.

She heard what sounded like a pack of rats running through the walls and stepped into the adjacent room. Ten screens were piled in the corner and she noticed a young female agent pulling a cord through the wall. A pile of black cable was piling up behind her. She shook her head and reached down towards her right ankle, grabbed a concealed item and stepped towards the wire.

"Step back."

Startled by her presence, the agent did so. She whipped the buck knife she held and severed the cord, then she turned to the agent. "Just cut them for Christ's sake."

The room was a complete mess when she turned and saw trash bins pass outside the room.

She stepped out to see a large collection of bins, which accounted for most of the available space. They were filled to the rim with phones, televisions, wiring, computers of various makes and sizes, laptop screens and speaker phones. She spoke over her intercom and said, "Mobile teams two and three, let's start loading up."

"Copy that."

Outside the White House gate, a dozen large black trucks started pulling in front of the main entrance. The agents in the trucks were tasked to collect the trash bins and remove them and the communication equipment from the building. They set to work while Courtney made her way to the Truman Balcony.

Three men were wrapping up the process of bolting the doors. The windows were secured to ensure President Drumpf would not be able to leave the White House grounds by climbing out a window.

That was the goal. She checked her watch and realized they had just four hours to complete the task at hand.

***

When the last of the trash bins left the building she stepped out into the cold to verify the convoy was ready to move.

Gerald, her top lieutenant, was sweaty and disheveled when he stepped forward. "Director Harper, any and all communication equipment has been removed from the White House. All entrances and exits, except for one, have been sealed."

"Excellent. Time for the next stage."

She barked another command into her intercom and the two waited by the front entrance. Two large vehicles turned off the road and made their way onto the White House grounds. They looked completely out of place, but given the Secret Service had already used all available vehicles, a short-term solution had been necessary. Two yellow school buses pulled in and parked outside the entrance to the building. Another team of fresh agents left the buses with either a vacuum or a bucket of cleaning products in hand.

"Let's get a move on. We have two hours to clean everything up."

Nearly fifty agents in all, junior members of the Secret Service team, exited the vehicles and stepped through the doorway.

The fresh crew began working enthusiastically, scurrying about to put everything back into place, remove debris and clean up the mess that remained in every office, hallway and gathering room.

One agent paused to smile at Courtney. She patted him on the back as he passed by. She then saw Gerald smiling at her from across the room.

"What?"

"I'm glad we're doing this. The entire country will be pleased."

"Glad you're so cheery."

"Who's going to break the news to the country?"

She sighed. "Speaker Bryan will take point on this primarily, but I'll be there to chime in too."

Her subordinate just shook his head.

"You think that's bad? I'm the one who's giving the news to Drumpf."

7:25 a.m.

The security detail snapped to attention when the door to the Lincoln bedroom opened. "Good morning Mr. President."

Drumpf barely acknowledged them as he turned in the hallway. His fingers fiddled with the edges of his coiffed hair. Every strand of hair was custom placed, aligned perfectly with his dark suit, crisp white shirt and red tie. Dashes of light reflected off his polished shoes as Drumpf began his walk down the hallway to the grand staircase.

President Drumpf was about to begin his first full day as commander in chief.

He turned his head slightly when he heard a secret service agent whisper something into his intercom. "Gentlemen," POTUS cleared his throat, "My chief of staff, his whereabouts?"

"Unknown sir."

"Press secretary, then?"

"Unaccounted for."

He paused to look at the agents. They remained silent. "Where's my breakfast?"

"Food will be provided after your meeting with the Director of Secret Service."

"That can wait. I'm bumping her to five today."

"Negative, sir." Drumpf stopped at the base of the staircase.

"I think you boys have this scenario reversed. I'm in charge." He grinned and pointed to his newly minted presidential lapel pin. "Now fetch my secretaries. I want them in the Oval Office immediately. I want to know why everyone is not here."

The security officers watched as Drumpf turned and took notice of his surroundings. It was obvious the décor and general presentation of the room had changed. A lopsided portrait of George Washington was directly in front of him and the walls to the left and right were pockmarked with holes. A coat of dust was visible on a nearby mantel. "What the…"

Drumpf stepped forward to look down one of the hallways. He looked up to the ceiling and saw what looked like gashes, the width of cable cords, zigzagging from one side to the next. He traced his fingers on a wood table and felt the dust rub between them. "What the hell happened here last night?" he demanded.

He turned and saw the men stand shoulder to shoulder. "That way, sir."

"What way?"

"The Oval Office. Director Harper is expecting you."

Drumpf cocked his head. He motioned with his hand as he approached them. "Out of my way, now." Drumpf's scowl darkened when he was inches from their faces.

"No sir." They did not move.

Drumpf's usual glow turned a shade darker, which gave him the appearance of a blood orange. He stormed down the hallway and raised his fingers. "I want answers! Where is everyone! What is the meaning of all this!"

His steps echoed on the marble floor as he stomped down the hall. He came to a hallway that lead in three directions. Appearing lost, he snapped his head from side to side.

"To your left, sir."

The president mumbled to himself as he shuffled down the hall. He then flung the doors open to the Oval Office.

Director Harper was seated behind the desk. A short man with glasses and a trimmed white beard stood beside her.

Drumpf slammed the doors but his escorts opened them immediately. He snapped his head when they did so. "Get out."

They turned to look at their boss and waited. Courtney

let the moment linger, then said, "Remain outside."

Drumpf turned to look at her. "They follow my orders from now on."

"No, they don't. Take a seat."

He stepped towards her. "Get out of my chair."

She shrugged her shoulders. "Suit yourself." She stood up and stepped around to the guest chairs before the President's desk. The short man cringed and walked around the opposite side to avoid what appeared to be an imminent physical confrontation.

The president remained standing. "I want answers. Why is the ground floor a disaster area?"

"Well, we did bring in a cleaning crew. I think, given everyone's workload, it looks pretty good."

"Shut up." He motioned to the man standing behind her. "Who are you?"

Courtney answered for him. "This is Dr. Rich Caliso, an advisor assigned and commissioned last night by the United States Congress."

"A doctor? I didn't invite him. Take your leave, little man."

Courtney grinned. "Well, that was easy. Dr. Caliso, would you agree with the Speaker of the House's assessment, and that of his colleagues in Congress?"

The man straightened up, taking confidence on some level from Courtney's direct manner and control of the situation. He nodded. "Yes I would. I concur."

"Thank you, sir. One of the gentlemen outside will escort you to the main entrance."

He grinned back at her, exhaled in relief, and took his leave. Courtney turned to face President Drumpf.

He crossed his arms. "I don't know who you think you are, but let me tell you something. You're fired."

Courtney grinned again and cleared her throat. "Let me bring you up to speed, sir. I don't report to you at present, nor will I for the duration of your term." She removed a piece of lint from her suit pants. "The Doctor you just met was a psychologist, a world-renowned one from what I hear. He was present at the hearings last night on the Hill."

"Like I care. Get out!"

"He's going to provide his final report to the Speaker of the House shortly. You see, when you went to bed, Congress convened in a special session and passed an emergency powers act that stripped you of any executive authority. It passed both houses by an overwhelming majority." She watched Drumpf unfold his arms, place them on the desk, his knuckles white with tension. For a moment he looked like an enraged gorilla ready to pounce. She added, "I guess, in hindsight, it would have made sense to make some friends up on the Hill."

"Leave! You're finished!"

"Take a seat," said Courtney.

His eyes appeared ready to pop out of their sockets when he stepped toward her. She reciprocated by revealing the Glock nine millimeter pistol fastened to her hip. "Step back, immediately."

Appearing shocked to see the weapon, he turned to find a phone, but found just a decapitated phone cord. He opened a drawer and found it empty. "I'm ordering you out. You brought a gun in here?"

"Please," she waved her hand, "part of my gear. Every agent carries one. As I was saying, the Secret Service's primary mission is to ensure the security and well-being of the President. Our authority, in this circumstance, is to ensure the security and well-being of the government. As the Doctor will point out to Congress, in this case, you may be president but you are not qualified to lead the country."

His fast stride carried him to the door he entered. When he opened them, two agents stood there to block his path. He slammed the door and then crossed the room to another door and opened it. Another pair of agents greeted him. "Son of a bitch!"

Courtney stood up and motioned for the doors to be closed. When they did Drumpf turned to face her from across the room. "We advised Congress that the best way to maintain that security and well-being was to ensure you had no outside contact with the world. We recommended the removal of any and all communication equipment from the grounds. Hence, the mess from last night."

"You crazy bitch."

"Just doing my job, sir. You won't find a computer, a phone, a cellular device, a satellite dish, anything. I'm authorized to confine you for the next four years to the interior of the White House."

He stomped towards the windows behind the desk and whipped open the curtains. What he saw gave him reason to step back.

His ass hit the desk a moment later.

A hundred suited men and women surrounded the length of the front side of the White House. Given the intercoms that dangled from their ears, they appeared to be Secret Service agents. Closer to the window, the remains of a satellite dish were lodged into the earth.

"Team front lawn, turn and wave, that's an order."

Drumpf's mouth dropped when a hundred agents turned to look towards the windows of the Oval Office and waved.

Drumpf's head dropped. Some time passed before Courtney continued. "I have another hundred agents covering every entry and exit point." She stepped around the desk. "That doctor you mocked will confirm to Congress that you are not, for example, mentally competent enough to manage our country's nuclear arsenal. You may know the executive branch of government does not need Congressional authority to act on what may or may not be an imminent nuclear threat."

"This is not happening! I was elected!"

"And in terms of the way you conducted yourself during the election cycle, members of Congress began to see how a Drumpf presidency represented a clear and present danger to the country. You're essentially under house arrest." She turned and stepped around the room. "Quite a nice house, when you think about it. It could be a lot worse."

"You stupid, ignorant, little whore."

"Well, when you're swimming in the Eisenhower pool,

you can thank me later."

He raised his head, turned to look at her, and chuckled for a brief moment. "You have no idea who you are dealing with. I'm in charge of the army for Christ's sake!"

"Nope, not at present. That now falls under the Speaker of the House's authority. A temporary circumstance is the phrase he used."

"So you orchestrated this?"

"I only follow orders, sir."

He shook his head in disbelief. "Then, it's a coup d'état. For God's sake, why... why are they doing this to me!"

She took a long breath, folder her arms and then leaned against the wall. "Where shall I begin? First off, you're a racist of the highest caliber, barring Muslims from the country and whatnot."

"Like I haven't heard that before."

"You're bad on the international front, simply because our neighbors will hate you, plus you have zero diplomatic experience. You want to start a commerce war with our number one trading partner and encourage militarization across most of the world. Our allies have no idea if you'll turn your back on them, and on the home front, you flip-flopped about the policies you would and would not support." She watched Drumpf's back stiffen. "Women have no idea if you're going to ban abortions. Thirty million people who have access to healthcare for the first time are going to get cut off when you tear Obamacare down." She watched his face contort with contempt. "Your economic advisors want to gut the Fed and pack that institution with a

32

bunch of laissez-faire cronies who will take orders from you and God knows who you'll finally nominate to the Supreme Court." She stood erect and stared down the man without even so much as a blink.

He started breathing heavily. He moved closer and she stepped back. Her hand reached down to untether the top flap of her waist holster.

"This is not happening!"

He swung around and in a quick motion picked up the Presidential chair over his head. He wavered, given the weight of it. He smashed it against the Oval Office windows. The sound echoed in the chamber of the room, but it simply bounced off, hit the credenza beneath it and crashed to the floor.

"Bulletproof windows, sir. Impenetrable."

His head swiveled as he looked for something else to use. He stormed to the right side of the room and removed the American flag from the base that held it. He pointed the heavy gold eagle at the top of the pole at her and moved closer. "Out of my way!"

She moved aside as he brandished it like a bayonetted rifle. "Back off!" he said, baring his teeth like a feral dog.

"You know, it's poor manners to let the flag touch the ground."

He rushed to the door. With one hand he opened it. Drumpf squared off with the agents who faced him. "Move!"

Courtney said, "Go ahead. Let him run around."

The men before Drumpf separated and he stormed past

them with his flag-draped spear in tow. He screamed as he ran down the hallway.

She walked behind him and watched him turn into an adjacent office. She heard him yell and it was followed by a loud bang. "Shit!" he screamed. She then saw Drumpf leave the room empty handed and stride towards the front of the building. She noticed his coiffed hair flop back and forth with each step he took.

His head swiveled in search of something. He crossed the room and picked up the Churchill bust on a nearby table.

Courtney stopped walking the moment Drumpf threw it at another window.

It hit the frame, bounced back and landed heavily by Drumpf's feet.

A significant dent was visible in Churchill's forehead. "Poor Winston," she said.

"Get away from me! All of you!" He ran further down the hall.

"Ronny!" cried a young woman standing at the top of the grand staircase. He turned to look at the first lady. Courtney turned the corner and saw Drumpf's couture-clad wife at the top of the stairs.

"Go back upstairs."

"Vhat is happening? Vhat is going on?" asked the First Lady.

"Just… try to find a way out!" He tore off down the hallway.

Courtney looked at her. "The Presidency," she

shrugged her shoulders, "It's a bitch."

For the next ten minutes, President Drumpf mustered all his might to smash windows, open doors or find a phone. He found all the windows were shatter proof and some welded shut. At one point, the tip of a French knife snapped when he used it to try to prod open a window. Doors to the outside were locked and multiple agents kept their eyes on him as he passed from one side of the building to the next.

His tie unknotted and clothes disheveled, Drumpf finally stumbled to the Oval Office and wiped his brow. She met him there and watched him sink into the presidential seat after he lifted it back into place. He stared at the desk before him, seeming both overwhelmed by the moment and infuriated by his sudden powerlessness.

She stood before him and waited, for what seemed like an hour for him to raise his eyes to look at her.

Courtney asked, "Are you finished?" He didn't so much as flinch. She spoke into her intercom. A moment later an agent brought her two items. She tossed one item on his desk: an unopened package of double-A batteries.

"Now what?"

She ignored the question and opened the other package which contained a pair of children's walkie talkies. They were the color of bright orange, which resembled his complexion. She turned them on, placed one on Drumpf's desk, and spoke into the other one in her hand. "Check one, check two." Her voice echoed in the other. "That will work. When you need us, speak into the provided walkie talkie and we'll accommodate you if we can."

He picked it up and looked confused.

"This represents your one and only communication device. Depress the side button and speak if you need us." She placed the walkie talkie in her jacket pocket and pointed to the door beside her. "Well, now you know where the kitchen is. We'll deliver food as usual, you won't be having any guests. Can you or the First Lady cook?"

He shook his head.

"Figures. I'll make sure some cook books are provided. God knows you'll have plenty of time to pick up a new hobby." She took a deep breath. "Well, that pretty much sums it all up. No one in, no one out, and you have a lovely home for the next four years. We'll have a hundred agents on guard inside and out at all times."

"Why are you doing this to me?"

She nodded in an empathetic manner. "I hear you, and I know this is hard on you. Here's your answer."

She retrieved her cell phone and dialed. A moment later she said, "Speaker Bryan? Yes, the grounds have been sealed and President Drumpf is aware of his circumstances. Dr. Caliso will be there shortly." She paused to ensure POTUS was looking at her.

She smiled. "Operation Abuela Vista is in full effect."

She watched his head rise. His eyes darted back and forth, seeming to look for an answer. She knew the second it hit him and his eyes locked onto hers.

When they did, she raised her hand, gave Drumpf the bird, and left the room.

"Now wait just a goddamn minute!"

She passed the agents outside the door. "Keep him in there."

Their shoulders squared before Drumpf appeared.

Courtney continued to walk and grinned when the President screamed and yelled as he tried to wrestle past the six-foot tall agents. She turned and caught a glimpse of the mayhem. It reminded her of a scene from *The Untouchables* when Al Capone, played by Robert De Niro, was restrained during the final court scene.

A moment later she left the building. She breathed in the cold air and then retrieved her cell phone to make another call. She smiled when her ailing father answered the phone.

"Hi dad. I have some news to share that will make your day."

Performance Anxiety

Presley Acuna

It's almost time.

Time to show it or blow it. I've got to relax. What is it about this guy that makes me so edgy? I feel nervous. It's like a tingle in the palms of my hands.

How's my hair? Damn, I'm puffy. I should have had it trimmed, but if they went too far, I might have ended up looking like a boy scout. Gotta go for that polished but not too polished, real person look. Too late for hair adjustments now.

Suit's OK – not flashy, just clean and pressed. But should I even be wearing a suit in this day and age? Politics are not what they used to be. No more flag pins on your lapel. Now it's t-shirts and baseball caps with your tag line emblazoned on them.

Mine's "No Scandal Randall".

It sucks, to be honest, barely fits on the hat, but it *does* fit on the hat, and it sends the right message, which is what counts. I've still got my integrity, unlike some of my

opponents. And I'm grounded in reality. I'm solid. I'm
real. Not like the others. I'm Senator Randall Bradley,
proud Son of the South, and I've got no gimmicks. I've got
to come across as the adult in the room. That's what
counts. That's the bottom line. For this face-off, more
than all the others, that has to count.

"Randall, you feeling the burn?"

That's Russell Cox, my campaign manager, bursting
through the door without so much as a knock. Christ, what
if I had been doing something weird right then? Wacking
off before this thing is definitely one way to let off some
steam. It was definitely in the back of my mind.

Relax, Bradley, you got this.

"Relax Randall. You got this," echoes Russell, weirdly
reading my mind. He comes over to the dressing table and
stands behind me. I know he's going to touch me now.
Bastard. Don't fucking touch me.

Randall lays a hand on my shoulder. It's worse that he's
so gentle about it. I try not to flinch. I would prefer a
strong hand, if you're gonna make the breach. A solid
grasp, goddammit.

Good Graces, I'm so tired. Tired of the sordid, venal
game that politics has become. I can hear you laughing
now. "LOL. What do you mean, 'has become', Bradley?"
Well, it has. There was always gamesmanship in the work
of getting elected -- that's as old as politics itself, perhaps
the *real* oldest profession, hmm. I wonder. But I digress.
Back in the day, politics was played by adults for adults with
a focus on the issues. It wasn't so much about sound bites
and cleverisms inevitably mistaken for truisms. It wasn't
entertainment.

"Do you want to go over your talking points again?"
asked Russell, squeezing my shoulder.

I shrug off his hand and swivel my chair to face him,

40

partially to hide the distaste I probably communicated in my reaction to his shoulder squeezing. Russell lets his hand drop and it hangs there in the air between us like a dead limb. I determinedly do not look at it. Neither does Russell.

"15 minutes to show time, sir," says one of the director's interns, popping in her head just long enough to say the words. We're both startled out of our strangeness. The whole thing is so strange. The entire planet is strange, if you ask me.

"No, Russ. Tonight won't be about the talking points."

Russell looks me over, brushes off a bit of lint from my jacket, and then something gives inside of him and he deflates. He walks around me, leans on the dressing table edge and stares at the ground. He pulls out an e-cigarette and lights up. I hate those fucking things. He should know that by now. Maybe it's his way of saying "Fuck you, Senator". I suddenly feel like laughing.

"Then what will it be about, Senator?" he asks, again seeming to mock me by repeating a word that just ran through my head. I stare at him, wondering. He blows some sweet smelling, faux smoke into the air. He looks tired. It's been a circus for both of us, I know.

"It'll be about demolition," I eventually say, surprising myself as much as it does Russell. He arches an eyebrow at me. A fly buzzes against a halogen bulb near my ear. Footsteps rumble past the dressing room door, muffled by the wooden barrier it provides. A tiny rivulet of my own sweat exudes from a pore on my back and snakes a long, slow and wet trail down my spine towards the elastic of my boxers.

"Russ, tonight's showdown will be about deconstructing my opponent before the eyes of the public."

"Unless Mister X does it to you first, Senator…"

I grunt, assenting, "He might, Russell. X portrays himself as something noble and yet innocent. That contrast in style to the usual grandstanding is his monkey wrench."

"And he'll be aiming it straight at your balls, sir."

"He will, but he'll have some salvos of my own to dodge too."

"I'll be watching from the trenches!" says Russell with a chuckle. A wrinkle of concern at the corners of his eyes. He speaks in bluster to me, but his thoughts are another matter.

My voice is worn gravel. "I've been on the road for so long, Russ, speaking 'til I have no voice, glad-handing flesh until my hands are numb, smiling into cameras and the overfed faces of the so-called, ordinary Americans who come out to hear me speak, God only knows why."

"Now there's a sound bite," snorts Russell.

"And yet all of my campaign's victories; all of my debate skills, all of my brilliant retorts, my ruthless dressing down of my various opponents, plus a few lucky breaks, and of course your campaign stratagems and the strength of our ground game forces, amount to nothing if I fail to defuse the enigmatic appeal of my final adversary tonight."

Russell responds, tuned into my diatribe, "You're the last of the Old Guard, sir". He crosses his legs at the ankles and settles into to listen to my rantings.

I nod, feeling a heat building within me. "And only I can do this. All the others, my brethren in office, have failed. Perhaps it's because of the dwindling skills of those who call themselves politicians. We are a dying faction, a discredited profession, damaged by decades of partisan politics and distorted law, corrupted by big money and ruled by intolerance. Finally the public saw and heard enough. They rebelled and despite all the weights we put in place against populist democracy, they overran the handicaps with large majorities and elected candidates outside of the ruling class."

"You mean we elected Donald Trump," finishes Russell, dryly.

"And that was only the beginning."

Russell nods, "He defied the odds."

"And defied the law, in the end. And a few civil rights," I answered sharply.

Russell pushed himself off the table edge and ambled towards the door. "But he got things done, Randall," he says looking back, "He made sweeping changes, for better or for worse. Amazingly, the judgment of history leans towards the view that he got things done. That he broke the partisan deadlock."

"At a high price, if you ask me. Yeah, some would say he broke eggs to make an omelet...," I respond.

"But you think what we got is scrambled eggs," quips Russell.

"Exactly. This is no longer the country I was born in," I reply, rubbing my cheeks. "I wonder if you could even call us a democracy anymore."

"A lot of people think it's more real the way it is now, sir. No more Electoral College. No more super-delegates. No more gerrymandering..."

"And no more primary process. Just this god-forsaken *2032 Presidential Smackdown*," I answered remorsefully.

"It's being called People Power," says Russell, reaching for the doorknob.

I snort my derision. "You mean television ratings power. The Presidential election process is now a televised reality show competition, Russ. There's even arm wrestling!"

We both fall into silence at this. Just as Russell is about to open the dressing room door, perhaps to cool down the air in the room, there's a knock. He opens it. The intern. "10 minutes, Senator."

I sigh, and sit upright, examining myself in the lighted mirror once more.

I hear the door shut behind me. The creak of Russell's well-worn shoes as he walks back over to me and looks me over. "Are you ready, sir?"

"Urm. Yes," I reply. I pat myself to make sure I have everything. "As ready as I will ever be."

* * *

We're walking along the backstage corridors, heading towards the podiums, to do our sound check. Russell in front, talking to the production assistant, making sure there's bottled water and notes ready for me.

As we walk, I reflect. I've travelled a long road to get here. Hard to believe I am even a finalist. The competition has been fierce.

The national contest for the Presidency begins with 50 candidates. One winner per state. The cream of their respective crops, selected from the local and regional face-offs and contests of skill and strength that preceded the national run-off. The idea of parties and primaries is long gone from our political process. It's all about personalities and public appeal now.

The nation has become fractured and factionalized; divided and conquered by the internet and its ability to empower every fringe group through social media and the panopticon of News-as-Entertainment, painting a cheap gloss of legitimacy over every insanity that bubbles up on the public stage, like fumaroles of rancid gas from the minds of the masses. The mindless mind of the masses.

California had been formidable. I was sure I was a goner against the Gippers. No one had foreseen the possibility of a candidate presenting him or herself as a team, in this case a team of clones of Ronald Reagan, who proposed a Presidency by Committee. It was seductive. The nation had considered it, but ultimately, the bickering among the Ronnies led to their downfall, especially when one of them decided to shoot all the others right on the debate stage last month. National Open Carry has its risks.

And I almost gave up the ghost in Massachusetts. The Kennedybot was an incredible simulacrum of the original Jack. An IE in a suit, looking nearly human but just an inch short of being totally convincing -- we had yet to fully jump the so called Uncanny Valley of revulsion when something looks human but is not-quite-there. And yet it sounded just as bold and appealing as our original cold war President, and with its encyclopedic access to the world's data banks, it could out-fact any opponent in a debate. People were creeped out but also excited. It was something different.

I finally resorted to throwing my glass of water at it, ultimately shorting it out. It had died in mid-sentence, blathering in moistened electronic confusion, "Ask not what this gantry can do for you, but what Yukons can do for... erk!"

The audience loved it and it gave me a huge boost in ratings, but I'll be fighting off that lawsuit for years, to be sure.

"We're here, Randall. Need you on the podium," says Russell, snapping me back to the moment.

I look around. The stage is vast, like an arena. More

than that. Like a circus, in the original, Latin sense; a Circus Maximus, as in ancient Rome, an arena for performances and contests – often to the death.

Enormous, wall-sized screens lay in silent menace behind me, ready to display high resolution images of Americana, and poignant bio-moments from each contestant's life. Faceless speakers, looming in stacks, stand to either side of the stage, positioned to blast the National Anthem and questions from the audience for all to hear. Stage monitors hang from above in front of the podiums, so as to display teleprompter texts to each contestant for the scripted parts of the coming telecast. And below them, the row of chairs and desks, for the moderators slash judges; a panoply of internet stars and Big News henchmen, ready to turn us on our spits before the public.

I hear a whirring sound like hummingbirds in the air.

Up there. Camera drones hover above, under computer control, riding to and fro like spiders traveling their invisible webs, as they are being tested. Come show time they will relentlessly race towards and zoom in on each contestant's face, capturing the smallest gestures and subtlest details, down to the rouge on our cheeks. There will be no escaping the scrutiny of the television audience.

"Senator Bradley, if you could step up to the podium and take your position, sir," says the production assistant, holding an iPad Wafer 20.0 and wearing a wireless headset. She barely bothers to notice whether I obey or not, and hurries off in search of something, or nothing.

I obey.

There's a rustle from the other side of the stage.

The curtains at the far wing part briefly and a man in gold tights, a cape and a mask steps forward followed by a small entourage. He is not tall, nor particularly muscular, and wears no air of arrogance as you might expect from one so brash as to wear a costume in public. He walks slowly, calmly and looks around the stage, taking it all in, much as I did. He sees me and aims himself in my direction.

The stage crew intercepts him and directs him toward his podium, positioned several feet to the right of my own.

He sidesteps them and comes toward me, extending a gloved hand.

Russell hurries over and whispers into my ear, "Cordial and relaxed, Randall. He's just a clown in a suit, but treat him like an honorable adversary."

Honor, I think to myself. Wasn't it Sophocles who once said, "I would rather fail with honor than succeed by fraud"? Is this man in a suit, the one and only Mister X, with the silver "X" emblazoned on his gold lamé chest, an honorable adversary or a fraud?

I am reminded of Neal Carson's sex change scandal. Now that one really took over the headlines. He had been the upstart Governor of Missouri, meteorically risen through the ranks. Then about halfway through his term, he had undergone gender change surgery, and emerged Governor Nellie Carson. She then proceeded to parlay the story of her decision into a parable of courage, character and grit after declaring her run for the Presidency.

It had traction with the public, until it was revealed that he, or she – it's so confusing -- had been a woman all along, who had, amazingly, faked being a man for the last 20 years. Neal had always been Nellie, and had faked her recent gender change surgery! It had been her undoing and was still being debated in the gossip and entertainment rags, with claims and counterclaims as to what was real and what was fabrication, and if it mattered at all what gender he or she was and what's so bad about lying anyway?

Now, there's just two candidates left in this race for the

Presidency: myself, and Mister X, the man in the mask, who claims to be a super hero, though he has performed no overt acts of super heroism to date. And yet he does wield power of a kind. He speaks with a calm confidence and a quiet gravitas that hypnotizes his audiences wherever he travels. He talks in parables about his alleged humble roots, without revealing any specifics, and describes them as the basis of his moral fiber. He has a good story, and a good costume, even if his super hero stint is a bit of a sideshow flamboyance.

And yet the country loves him. Of all the clowns in the clown-car, blowing their klaxons, he has struck the most disarming note to a nation tired of broken promises and empty histrionics. His level voiced earnestness quiets the impulse to ridicule, and instead, inspires a certain slack jawed imagining and moment of wonder. Could he be a hero to this broken country? God knows, the country needs one. Even I have felt it.

I look at him, inches away now, and wonder about the costume. Is there a subtle juxtaposition going on there? Could that be his magic? The nation has had its forays of putting Cowboys, Soldiers, Actors and Rock Stars into the Oval Office. All have crumpled, either victims of their own narcissism, or once faced with the pressures and complexities of world leadership, have shown themselves to be nothing more than woefully inadequate figureheads. Yes, I wonder about the costume. The costume leads us to wonder about the man behind the mask. Does it *focus* us on the man behind the mask too, by some perverse design of intent?

I sigh. *Who knows?* All I know is that it's boiled down now, reduced to a fine glacé. A contest of two extremes: myself, the last establishment politician, and Mister X, the nation's first super hero. Here we are, scheduled to compete on the national stage, in a series of contests, verbal and physical, to determine who truly has the mettle, the mind, the imagination and the methods that can win over the hearts and minds of America.

I step down from my podium and meet him halfway.

"A pleasure to see you again, Senator," says Mister X, extending a gloved hand in my direction.

After a moment's hesitation, I extend my naked hand, and clasp his. It's small. He squeezes. I squeeze back and we lock eyes. The material of his glove feels soft, like suede, and I realize that clasping his hand is not unlike holding a hamster. I almost expect to feel a rapid, small heartbeat. I pull back, but keep it slow, so as to not show my disdain.

We flash teeth at each other.

"May the best man win, Mister X," I say to my caped opponent.

"X. You can just call me X, when we're not on stage, Senator."

I nod, bemused, "Randall. But don't you have a real name? Like, a person's name?"

"No," he responds flatly, unblinking.

"Gentlemen, please take your positions. 2 minutes to show time," says another Production Assistant.

Our private moment is broken by the needs of the larger moment. We head to our respective podiums. Russell and a small knot of handlers are waiting for me there. Russell pats me down and straightens my tie; a young woman hits me with a powder puff right in the kisser. Another brushes off any signs of powder from my clothing. A microphone is clipped into my lapel. An earpiece is plugged into my ear. A comb across my hair and then like magic, they are gone and the footlights turn up. I hear more than see the rank of moderators come into the arena and taking their seats just beyond the apron of the stage.

The screens behind me flicker on and the stage glows bright with their imagery, but the teleprompter is flashing "Don't Look Behind You! Look At The Cameras!" The alluded to cameras float in the black abyss before us on cranes and dollies, where the audience will soon be, red LEDs showing their positions in the darkness. A man with a headset and mic standing in front of the moderators, counts down with his fingers as the Teleprompters also do, and at zero, gives us the thumbs up and disappears. Just then, patriotic music swells from the giant speakers on either side as a montage of red, white and blue, LED projected light patterns dance across and all around the stage.

A deep baritone announcer's voice suddenly fills the space, "Ladies and Gentlemen, welcome back to *The 2032 Presidential Smackdown*, brought to you by the Anheuser-Busch Companies, makers of America™ beer, and the International Bottled Water Association, your one source for the only drinking water you can trust!"

Huge applause from the audience as the floor behind the moderators smoothly parts and an enormous, 1,500 person seating area rises from below on silent hydraulics, filled with this week's live audience, selected by internet lottery at random from a pool of national applicants, travel and lodging not included.

The applause subsides and from one of the wings of the stage steps the smartly dressed *Smackdown* host, Chuck Hazzard.

"Welcome back, America, to *The 2032 Presidential Smackdown*," he chortles, to another wave of applause.

The music subsides and he takes center stage. My smile is firmly pasted on and I wait for my cue. X is waving to the crowd already. I feel a nibble of resentment over that.

Show a little class, caped crusader!

"Last week, the *Smackdown* gripped the nation, as Kentucky's finalist, Aladdin Shane, failed to survive the Dreadmill, leaving our two remaining contestants for the Nation's highest office, Senator Randall Bradley and the mysterious Mister X!"

I wave, on cue.

"That was amazing, wasn't it, folks? I'm happy to report that Mr. Shane is recovering nicely and will soon be released from the hospital. Mr. Shane, if you are watching, we just want to tell you that you are truly an entertainer, and probably a great statesman too! Give it up for Aladdin Shane, people!"

More applause.

"Well, strap yourselves in, America. It's time for the ride of your lives. The final showdown! Let's do this! Whoo!"

* * *

"I'm ready, Chuck," I say to the M.C., exhausted and humiliated, after two hours of enduring challenges ranging from quiz games, to physical contests, to demonstrations of dexterity, and now, finally, an actual Q&A session with the show's moderators, while the audience waits, prepared to score the results on their hand held reaction meters.

"Senator Bradley," begins Leillana Gidry of POTUSPicker.com, "If you were given the power to change one law on the Federal books, what law would that be, and how would you change it?

I feel the pressure to answer quickly – the tick tock sound effect being played from the stage speakers doesn't help - even though a ridiculous question like that might take days or even weeks to contemplate and answer with some semblance of responsibility. But too much delay in responding won't play well on this show, so I pull one out of my ass and hope for the best.

"I would declare term limits for all people in Congress," I answer. "President Trump did away with a lot of the process and regulations that stood in the way of getting elected to National office, but he left that one out. I would finish what he started."

The audience starts to hoot, and rewards me with a decent amount of applause. That was one heckuva good answer for improvised B.S., if I do say so myself.

Hazzard looks at me and flashes an approving smile, then turns to the audience and goads them, "Come on, come on, people. That's a very scandalous proposal from Senator 'No Scandal' Randall, isn't it? What do you really think, people? Let's hear it!"

Again, decent cheering and applause. Giant analog meters displayed on the screens behind me show the audience response. I take a look. 63 points. Not bad but not great.

Now it's Mister X's turn. He's been giving me a licking in all the physical challenge rounds so far. My only winning strategy is to win at all the verbal contests. The little guy is nimble and actually appears to be flying at times, especially during that Grab-a-Globe competition. We had to traverse a room by swinging from globe-shaped handholds hanging from a downward slanted ceiling. The idea was you moved from knob to knob, trying to get to the other side before your opponent, but being careful to not let your speed overtake you, or else you would fall. I didn't fall, but I could not overtake X, who seemed to defy gravity.

"Mister X," asks Leillana, as X confidently stands there,

hands on his hips, in his gold tights, cape furling slightly. "What is your answer to the question? What law would you change?"

The tick tock sound effect fills the arena and the camera drones hover in close to X's face. He's calm as a god dammed sphinx and even darts his eyes left and right, for comic effect. And then he says, "America, people of America, I would make all legislation subject to national ballots. In other words, all new laws or changes to laws would be subject to a national ballot. No more Congress. Just you and your vote."

What? There's a stunned silence. I think it's mostly due to people just not getting it. America is not used to this type of talk. There's a smattering of uncertain claps and a murmur grows through the crowd. A couple of woops here and there.

Mister X keeps going, "That way, each and every one of us would be citizen super-heroes. Don't you see? Each and every one of us would be directly responsible for defining the laws of the land. No middle men. Pure Democracy, for everyone."

The final deconstruction of our Government. I realize my own words to Russell, about demolition, spoken earlier in the evening, have become prophetic.

The camera drones swivel abruptly and turn their electronic eyes onto the audience. Somebody must be shouting orders in the control room, I'm sure. This is unexpected. They scan the ranks of dumbfounded faces with their faceless lenses. I gaze at the screens behind me. The drones are zooming in on people looking around the room, evaluating each other, as if for the first time.

I know what they're thinking. They're imagining pitting their vote against that foreign looking person in the next row, or that fat fuck across the aisle, or that dude wearing that stupid Ghostbusters shirt, and over there that buttoned down, born-again putz, and what about those gun-nuts and skin-heads sitting over there? They get to vote too?

The looks of bewilderment slowly morph into expressions of fear and hate. Someone boos. It catches on like fire. Like wildfire. In seconds the entire place is booing and hissing at Mister X. Mister X looks bewildered, and turns his head in my direction, as if for answers.

Hazzard looks to the wings for instructions and nods. The reaction meters are showing low 20's for X's answer and the screens suddenly flicker and switch to an image of a can of America™ beer with a furling flag behind it. A beer ad plays. The audience is not subsumed.

"Ladies and Gentlemen, it's time for a station break!" says Hazzard with gold plated glee, shouting a little to be heard above the growing audience unrest. "We'll be right back after this message from our sponsors. Stay tuned for more *2032 Presidential Smackdown* when we return!

The screen goes dark and the music stops. Hazzard, now serious, shouts into the crowd, "Folks please remain calm. Let's not forget, it's just a show."

"Shut up, you carnival barker!" someone shouts back from the audience.

"Hey, you, why don't you shut up?"

"Fuck you, you fucking Nazi."

That last outburst sets off the room and soon the entire audience is trying to shout each other down or insulting each other with every possible derogatory slur. Very quickly, objects are being thrown and people are lunging at each other and wrestling on the ground.

Hazzard pleads with the crowd to no avail. The lights come on, robbing the room of its largess. It's just an ugly auditorium now, filled with ugly people. The Moderators make for the exits without so much as a nod in our direction.

I unclip my mic and leave it on the podium. I start to walk towards Mister X's podium. He sees what I am doing and does the same. He looks hesitant, for the first time since I have known of him.

Suddenly, the television camera LEDs come on again. I catch their red glare from the corner of my eye but don't bother looking. I just know. Someone has forgotten to cancel the broadcast and the station break has ended, allowing the viewing public to have an unfettered view of the growing chaos in the room.

I look down at Mister X. He's shorter than me. The room is getting noisier.

"Why the X?" I ask. He stares at me, and blinks.

"What? None of that matters, right now, Senator. What should we do about this situation?"

"I don't know. You started it. Make a speech or something."

He looks out at the crowd, climbing over their seats to get at each other. Hazzard has completely disappeared. The cameras roam the room, greedily capturing the mayhem for the national television audience. X and I stand alone, face to face, amidst the noise and clatter.

"We both started it," he says. "We both allowed it to get this way. Ourselves and all the others in this race."

"I don't walk around in gold tights, X."

"But don't you see? I thought you might get it. The costume is my way of *exposing* disguises. The point is people like you are wearing the costume. The business suit. The grey sideburns. The gravely voice speaking sweet little lies. People don't want that wallpaper anymore. They deserve better."

I cross my arms. "Indeed they do, X, we're in agreement there. But they can't tell what's good for them. They don't have the skills anymore. They need leaders to guide them. Seasoned leaders. Statesmen. Otherwise, they just go after the shiny objects. Like you."

A shiny object lands on the stage, thrown from the seats below, just missing Mister X. He ignores it, "I'm more than just a shiny object, Senator. I'm a grass roots phenomenon."

I laugh at that.

He steps closer, evidently peeved. "Whatever you might think of me, I offer something better. Something honest. Something fresh. Your class of leaders are bought and sold by corporations."

I shake my head, feeling impatient. "Not anymore. That's all gone to hell, and you know it. Politics has devolved into just another perverted form of entertainment. I am this country's last best hope of getting back to sanity."

X actually pokes me in the chest. "How? By restoring the former status quo? Gerrymandering, pork, filibustering?"

I shove his hand away. "No, by using my experience and knowledge of government and law..."

"That's a load of crap."

I feel my blood rising. "I'll tell you what is a load of crap. That idea you just pitched into the crowd. Look at them now! Is that your idea of grass roots?"

X looks down at the boiling audience. Fistfights are breaking out all over the room and many people lay crumpled on the ground, unconscious or crying, or moaning in pain. No one is attempting to control the disruption, though sirens can be heard in the distance. He looks back to me, with angry eyes, as if, somehow, I am to

56

blame.

That pisses me off and I bark at him, "The fact is the United States of America is anything but united in what it thinks about anything. We're too big of a country, with too many factions and too much distance between us all. We're not connected to each other anymore. There's no national identity. We're all sitting in darkened rooms with just a television monitor as our window into the world, feeding us trash and vaudeville. We don't talk to each other except in internet chat rooms. We unfriend anyone whose opinion we don't like. We've been taught by the Trump years to loath and fear anybody different from us. We're all xenophobes. Is that what that fucking X on your chest stands for?"

Suddenly, Mister X's eyes grow wide and his face reddens. With inhuman speed he lunges at me, a blur of gold foiled anger and vitriol. He moves too quickly for me to avoid his assault and within seconds he has his hands around my neck and I stumble, trying frantically to not fall to the ground.

We have fully devolved into monsters and madmen, I think to myself as I struggle to pry the slippery little guy off of me. Every last person in this auditorium, including the two finalists for the Presidency, are trying to kill each other.

Fascinating.

I finally manage to pry him off and lift him over my head, amazed at how light he is. *I guess that explains how he won the Grab-a-Globe competition, heh*. He squirms and waves his arms and legs wildly, trying to throw me off balance. I'm no spring chicken so I can't do this for long. What do I do with this raving bon bon?

Pivoting on the stage, my eyes finally settle on the writhing melee of the audience and I decide.

With one enormous surge of effort, I cock my arms back and heave Mister X forward into the air, and send him sailing, like the super hero he imagines himself to be, into the thick of the audience below. He lands on them, like a teenage boy throwing himself into a mosh pit, and is immediately consumed by the hands and arms of the people beneath him, who are annoyed and angry at his intrusion, or perhaps his words, who can tell?

He cries out as he is enveloped by the bodies of the crowd, a dogpile of humanity smothering the gold lame of his sudden presence among them, and then he is gone. I can no longer see him or hear him.

* * *

It finally ends, as all things do. Police arrive. Medical teams cart away the injured. Reporters appear, soberly narrating their version of what just happened, as the cameras pan the wreckage of *The 2032 Presidential Smackdown*. It certainly was that. Probably a ratings blockbuster. No doubt, it will set a new standard for action entertainment in modern American politics.

All the while, I sit on the edge of the stage, watching civilization trying to re-assert itself, going through the motions, following orders, assuming the waters will recede once again. Cox appears from the wings and ambles over, e-cig in hand. He looks completely unruffled by what has just occurred. He crouches and sits, joining me as we watch the activities below.

He turns his head to look at me, hands me a comb, pats me on the back and says, "I guess you won, Mr. President."

THE END

Presley Acuna

Percussion Publishing invites you preview to Presley Acuna's top rated, Apocalyptic Thriller:

In the year 2020, a Christ-like figure grows in power and influence, challenging human institutions and the geo-political balance. Only a doubting priest and a secret hidden by the Vatican for millennia can stop him.

"The Bottom Line: A glorious end-times religious thriller like you've never read before. Newcomer Presley Acuna's debut novel should be placed near the top of your reading queue."
—**BestThrillers.com**

Available Now on Amazon and Kindle

Presley Acuna

Georgia, near the Azerbaijan border

The lowlands south of Tbilisi and north of Tobuz and the Kura River were a fertile but featureless expanse of agricultural plantations and barbed wire. This was the border between the Islamic republic of Azerbaijan and the war-torn, Christian nation of Georgia. A movement, which called itself the Azerbaijan Popular Front, had gained strength in recent years, recruiting heavily from the semi-autonomous Western territories of Russia, the fledgling Slavic nations splintered off during the 1990's from the long extinct Soviet Union, and the more recently created autonomous regions of war ravaged Afghanistan, Iraq and Iran. From this vast swath of disaffected peoples, the APF had forged a multi-national Islamic alliance under the command of the previously unknown guerrilla leader, Eli Tubasi.

Tubasi, a former petroleum worker and a minor official in the Azerbaijan capital city of Baku, had risen to power with the overthrow of the dictator, Ali Surat Mutaliyov. He was now the primary spokesman and leader of the APF, though this movement was now extended far beyond its original borders. In the years following the dissolution of the Soviet Union, Georgia had been hard pressed to remain intact. In addition to the pressures placed upon it by the APF, there were several autonomous regions within its borders, all of which were engaged in constant struggles for expansion and military gain against the former parent nation.

Georgia was also the site of numerous stockpiles of H.E.U., or highly enriched uranium -- an uncomfortable legacy from the days of the U.S.S.R. Securing these stockpiles during this period of military conflict and unpaid salaries was a challenge that was, frankly, not being met. In the last decade, several individuals peddling nuclear material stolen from the former Soviet Union, had been arrested in Europe and the Middle East, but so far there had been no confirmed cases of countries or terrorist groups obtaining the ingredients for making a bomb through such thefts. It was only a matter of time before such a thing would come to pass.

"The reactor guards work in 24 hour shifts, al-Sayyab." said General Julian Serbenko, a veteran of the former Soviet Union's security force.

"Shhhh! They'll hear you!" whispered Ibn al-Sayyab, clad in robes, a camouflage parka and a weapons belt, his breath a vapor, as he crouched behind a soot smudged brick wall, alongside the bedraggled and unshaven Russian General. The weather beaten building which they regarded in the moonless darkness was not one hour from the capital city of Tbilisi but they may as well have been in Siberia for all the life that could be discerned here. It was also only a short drive to the border. This amazed al-Sayyab. Leave it to the Russians to build a nuclear power plant less than one half hour from the frontier. But then again, in the old days, it wasn't the frontier.

One lonely spotlight illuminated the rusting metal doorway. It was a decrepit monument to the lost heyday of Soviet science. The entrance to the storage compound of Georgia's largest -- and fully non-operational -- nuclear reactor.

The General ignored al-Sayyab's comment. "At precisely 1:17 AM both guards will be at the opposite side of the building engaged in a weapons sale. It is a ruse entirely for your benefit."

"A clever plan, General Serbenko. Who would expect one illegal activity to camouflage another?" The Persian nodded approvingly. "Tubasi will be pleased."

"*Da*, perhaps he will. And you have the payment?"

"My men, beyond the ridge, have the package. After we have the H.E.U. you will receive it."

"*Otlichno*. We begin in five minutes. Signal your men."

al-Sayyab turned, and hurled a few stones over the ridge behind them. He was answered with a faint, short whistle. Shortly thereafter another camouflage clad figure appeared.

"Ah, Herif. Good," nodded al-Sayyab as he was handed something. al-Sayyab and Herif exchanged whispers. Serbenko checked his weapon, his back against the brick wall. Herif ran off.

"Two minutes," growled the General softly, his voice like gravel in the darkness.

They were an unlikely pairing. Tubasi's APF machinations had thrown them together for this raid -- and each had much to gain -- but afterwards they would return to their usual condition of mistrust and mutual hatred.

They waited, barely breathing.

From the other side of the building could be heard the rumble of an approaching truck. The crunching sound of the guard's footfalls quickly followed.

Serbenko poked the Persian hard with his finger, "The ruse has begun. Go!"

al-Sayyab ran in a low crouch to the base of the storage compound's doorway. He extracted a small package from the confines of his robe. Looking back for an instant, he spotted the General peering around the brick wall ready to provide cover if it was needed. al-Sayyab hoped it was not. These Russians were the worst kind of infidel traitors. They would sell their mothers.

He worked the plasticized PETN compound into the door frame and around the locking mechanism, and then embedded a radio controlled blasting cap into the plastic around the lock. Satisfied with his work he ran back to the protection of the brick wall.

"Ready, Comrade Serbenko."

"GENERAL Serbenko."

"EX-General Serbenko."

Serbenko smiled coldly. "I should kill you now and leave your worthless body here for the locals to find, you overzealous camel dropping."

"Poetic, comrade, but much as I might enjoy trading insults with you, the time has come for action."

And with that, al-Sayyab pressed the button on the radio detonator he exposed from under his robes.

FOOM!

The door shuddered and blew inwards in a cloud of dust and noise.

"The explosive works well, *vidal?*" commented the General proudly.

"*Chraa,*" al-Sayyab grunted, disinterested, and waved his associates on. Like wraiths they rose from their hiding places and cautiously made their way toward the entrance.

As they approached the storage facility, the two guards who should have been guarding the doorway suddenly came charging forth from opposite corners of the building with their guns blazing. The racket was curtailed abruptly by the "thup thup" of semi-automatic, silenced weapons blasting holes in the two hapless sentries. They fell face first into the dirt in a simultaneous stumbling motion, and lay inert.

"*Idioty,*" muttered the General.

al-Sayyab beckoned his man forward. The raiding party entered the facility.

"Ah, vintage fifties Empire. What an antique," remarked Serbenko, looking around disgustedly, as they scanned the gloomy interior.

"*Yala!*" shouted al-Sayyab to his men and gestured at an interior vault door.

Several of the raiders converged on the doorway and began to don radiation suits from a nearby rack.

When they were ready, three of the raiders entered the room, carrying a very large, long duffel bag. They opened the bag to reveal a lead-lined, carbon graphite casing with a shaped interior exactly matching the dimensions of a nuclear fuel rod.

Following their training, which Serbenko had provided, the three raiders set about working the winch controls within the vault room to lift out one of several nuclear fuel assemblies which lay submerged in the deuterium filled containment pool. Once they had one of the assemblies positioned over a graphite palette, they extracted one of the rods and quickly placed it inside the portable casing they had brought. They worked rapidly and soon the casing was back in the duffel bag and they were out of the vault.

As soon as they had shed the heavy protective garments and re-donned their winter gear, six APF men lifted the duffel bag and, with a signal from al-Sayyab, proceeded out of the containment building into the cold, Georgian winter. Ahead, a convoy of shuttered headlights abruptly blazed into brightness, as more of al-Sayyab's troupe came forward to assist their comrades.

al-Sayyab and Serbenko stood watching for a few moments. Then they turned toward each other.

"Mission accomplished, comrade," said al-Sayyab with a bow. As he came up from his bent position, he revealed a small automatic weapon.

Serbenko raised an eyebrow and coolly assessed the weapon that was aimed at his heart. "A 9x18 Makarov. Probably Bulgarian from the looks of it. Very impressive, camel herder."

"You will cease calling me that, infidel."

"*Idioty!* Didn't you think I would expect this from the sorry likes of you?" sneered Serbenko as he slashed his arm in a wide arc. A long blade emerged from his sleeve, propelled by centrifugal force, and sliced its way through the air where al-Sayyab's neck formerly occupied space.

al-Sayyab was on the ground a few feet away, "I did indeed expect that much of you, EX-General. Now you will be more than EX, you will be altogether EX-tinct!" al-Sayyab fired his pistol from the ground and the Russian crumpled like a heavy pillar to the ground, as he spat out a curse.

"*Chort!*"

That was his last word.

As al-Sayyab stood, he could hear distant sirens and shouting voices. *As usual, the Russian Calvary -- far too late -- probably Serbenko's fail-safe backup*, he thought to himself.

"*Ilaa l-liqaa', sharmute,*" he said with a grim laugh to the General's corpse, bidding his leave, and walking calmly toward the waiting convoy of trucks.

"To the frontier," he ordered quietly to his driver, feeling extraordinarily calm. Soon the *Jihad* would have its flaming sword to wield against the Zionists and imperialist infidels. Soon the everlasting struggle between Ishmael and Isaac, the sons of Abraham, would come to a culmination and justice would be done once and for all time. He would receive his blessing from Tubasi back in Baku. Then there would be only one more gesture to make.

Percussion Publishing invites you preview to Kendall Smith's 5-star rated thriller:

When estranged brothers John and Alan Devenger discover their grandfather has bequeathed them a secret legacy that got their father killed, they want no part of it ct first. But even as they bury their beloved relative, sinister forces are at work. A murderous conspiracy is unfolding that only the brothers can stop — and only if they can overlook a lifetime of resentment to act as one.

Hidden from the world within the chambers of a private Swiss bank are the spoils of war their grandfather, a World War Two hero, claimed for himself. By the time John and Alan learn the shocking truth of what's contained in Vault 21-12, they will either be bonded for life… or they'll be dead.

Available Now on Amazon and Kindle

Kendall Smith

Chapter 2

Ridgewood, New Jersey

The Lincoln town car pulled up to the entrance of Valley Hospital. Alan's eyes focused on the doors and his fingers tapped the door panel. He was ready to jump.

"Alan?" his driver asked tentatively.

"Yes?"

"I hope he's alright, I met him a year ago when I dropped you off in Upper Saddle River."

Alan nodded. "Thanks, I appreciate that."

"He seemed like a pretty strong guy. He'll get through this."

Alan nodded and exhaled slowly before he grabbed the door handle. He was outside a moment later. A cold breeze caught his attention before he heard the automated doors swoosh open before him. He checked his watch: it was 10:15 a.m. *Damn tunnel traffic.*

He stepped inside and made eye contact with the receptionist.

The woman smiled before she noticed the look on Alan's face. "Everett Devenger, where is he?"

She looked down at computer. "Intensive care, room 210-B. Down the hall there." She pointed.

"Thank you." Alan's shoes squeaked against the linoleum floor. A hundred yards down from reception were two swinging doors. He ignored a sign that read 'Passes required,' and walked by air respirators and what looked like a dialysis machine.

He turned a corner to see a waiting room and four relatives looking back at him. The look on their faces did nothing to lift Alan's spirits. The pace of his steps shortened as aunt Jenny stepped forward to embrace him.

"Jenny, what happened?" He bear-hugged her and reached up to feel her shoulders. She slouched into his chest. She looked up and shook her head, not knowing what to say or how to respond.

He felt another relative pat him on the back. "He's not doing well my dear," said Jenny. "I'm sure he'll be happy to see you but I think this is it, Alan."

"Jesus." He stepped back and sighed. His uncle moved to embrace him. Alan felt comforted by the strong hug. "What did the doctors say?"

His cousin stepped forward. "I'm glad you made it, Alan. He's holding on, as long as he can."

"The doctors, what's the word please?"

Alan saw the sad look on their faces but no one responded.

The nonverbal answers did not sit well with him. "Okay then, I have to see him."

"He's at the end of the hall to the right," said Jenny. She reached out and put her hand on his arm. "Alan," she said, "he's fragile, do you understand?"

Alan stopped and turned to look at her. "Okay, just please find me the doctor will you?" He turned to walk down the hall.

He noticed he had twenty yards to walk. His pace slowed when he thought about what Everett meant to him. He was a hero to him, literally and figuratively, given his honorable service during World War Two and his role as a father figure. Every time he took one step forward his mind replayed another role his grandfather played in his life. He was his role model and the dad he never had. The few faint memories he had of his father, before he passed away, were trivial when compared to the influence his grandfather played in his life.

He thought about his career, his success and the wealth that afforded Alan's education as well as half a dozen other siblings and cousins. He owed everything to Everett.

Halfway down the hallway, he felt pangs of frustration slow him down. *This is not happening, not now.* He pondered Jenny's reaction on the phone. Perhaps she was overreacting. Maybe Everett still had a chance... It could be another false alarm.

He noticed beams of sunlight extend from the room where Everett was located and took a deep breath. He paused and took comfort in the moment and saw it as a sign of hope.

The optimism he felt evaporated when he saw the silhouette of the man appear in the doorway. The man wore glasses, a black jacket and a short white collar.

"Are you here to see Everett?"

"I am."

The priest held a bible in one hand, and the other came to a rest on Alan s shoulder. "He has made his peace with

God. Try to make him as comfortable as possible my son."

Alan froze and listened to the priest's steps fade away behind him.

He could not produce words or thoughts. Alan forced a step forward and turned around the corner of the doorframe.

He stopped in mid stride when he saw his grandfather lying in the bed. Before he heard the heart monitor register a second heartbeat, he knew it was the end.

The once-strong man was already pale as death. The color of his skin seemed lighter in color, almost yellowish in nature and thin. His grey mane of hair was tossed about and his hands just sat there, without a trace of strength or life. Tubes extended from his arms, chest and nose in a variety of directions and he heard the man's heart beep echo from the sound of a machine.

It was the first time in Alan's life he saw his grandfather possess so little of it.

He stepped forward to the side of the bed. Alan's eyes moistened but he fought the urge to cry and leaned forward. "Grandpa."

His blood-shot eyes opened and turned to see his grandson. They lingered there for what seemed like an eternity to Alan. He tried to catch his breath and sputtered a word before waving him closer.

"Al... Alan my boy. I'm sorry you have to see me..." His words faded.

Alan stepped closer and grabbed his grandfather's lukewarm hand. "I'm so sorry this happened. I——." Alan told himself to remain positive. "Did the doctors say when they think you'll get out of here? Back home?"

His grandfather shook his head. "I'm afraid... that's not going to happen son. But I'm so happy you are here."

Alan's chest went numb when he heard the words. "Everett, you had one of these before, you were strong then and you're strong now." He looked down and noticed the barrel chest of Everett Devenger lift slowly in a cumbersome fashion.

His grandfather's grip tightened, surprising Alan for a moment. "You...you've been good to me." His eyes glazed over for a moment.

Alan bit his lip and used his hand to rub the side of his Grandfather's face. He was still conscious and he heard him let out a sigh.

"I cherish the moment we came down that hill together in Austria. I'll never forget it."

Alan furrowed his brow. "Everett, try to rest. We've never been to Austria together, it's okay."

"You know, outside of Feldkirch. We were there."

Alan shook his head but didn't want to upset the man. "Oh. Okay."

"Your father. He would have been proud of you. I'm proud of you. You've made a good life for yourself." He saw him smile for a brief second. "Now just get a gal, won't you?"

Alan smiled and thought about the last few girlfriends in his life. They were special in their own unique ways, but none stood out as his soul mate. "I'll keep looking, you know I will."

Alan's mind filled with the memories of his deceased father, and the role Everett had played when things took a turn for the worse during his childhood. He missed those moments, as if they were long lost friends, and turned his attention back to his grandfather. "You were there for me Everett. You were great." The emotion he felt came to the surface and materialized when tears fell from his eyes. Alan pursed his lips together to hide the emotion.

Everett tilted his head to get a good look at his grandson. "I'm sorry."

"You have nothing to be——."

"I'm sorry about your father. I'm sorry I got him involved. It was my fault."

"It was an accident, my father and the car. Don't say that."

"He didn't die the way I told you, he was in Switzerland. He——." Everett tried to sit up but could not muster the strength. Alan heard the heart monitor quicken in pace. "Listen. Your father was getting something for me... for him... in Switzerland." He coughed, and wheezed before saying, "They killed him. It was no accident. I know it for a fact. You have to be careful. I left you the details. I should have talked to you and John. It's in your hands now."

The heart monitor raced as Alan processed the information. *Murder... his half-brother... Switzerland.* When he stopped shaking his head he looked down at the man before him and realized how fragile Everett was. He refused to let the words get to him.

Everett stared at him with intensity. "Be good to your brother, Alan, be good to him."

The pace of the heart monitor slowed but it did not stop. "Everett, talk to me. Did something really happen over there?" There was no response. He just sat there, seeming to struggle with each breath.

The guilt Alan felt was of his own making. He wanted to shake the man awake. *Tell me about my father, what happened, why John of all people, how do you know it was not a car accident?*

Alan took a seat beside the bed. The minutes passed by and still there was no sign of consciousness from Everett.

He could not help but wrap his head around what Everett told him. He thought about his father, and the fact he died when he was eight years old. From what he was told, there was no mystery. It was a car accident, pure and simple.

He turned when he heard the squeak of someone's shoes outside in the hallway.

A moment later he made eye contact with a relative he had not spoken to in several years. Standing before him was his estranged half-brother, John. He watched his response to the sight of Everett in the bed. Any flutter of hope his half-brother harbored evaporated when he saw the man. It looked like a mirror image of what Alan felt ten minutes prior.

His cynical nature thought the moment was ironic. His grandfather's fate represented the only thing he had in common with his half-brother.

"Is he conscious?" John whispered.

Alan rose from the chair and crossed his arms. "I'd think about what you want to tell him, but most of all, listen. He mentioned—."

John walked past his Alan and went to the bed. His scarf draped across the handrail and he placed his hand to his grandfather's forehead. Pursing his lips, he reached out to touch the man's cheek. His other hand gripped Everett's wrist, as if he were feeling for a pulse.

"Hey… grandpa. It's John. Can you hear me?"

Alan walked beside him. John provided Alan with a scowl and then turned back to the bed. "Can you give me a moment with him?"

Alan paused and turned to look at John. "Come again? I thought—."

"Please, Alan." John's pleading tone expressed more than the words ever could.

Alan stepped away and exited the room.

At that moment, Everett drew a deep breath through wheezing lungs, and looked up to see John.

"Hey, grandpa."

"John?"

"It's me. What happened?"

"It doesn't matter." There was a long pause before he said. "You're here… you're here."

"Are you in pain? What can I do to help?"

His grandfather smirked for a moment, seeming to laugh. "Listen to me, John." His head rolled back on the pillow, and John moved closer. "You and your brother, you're the only men left in this family. I mean, real men, who've achieved something. You have each other. You have that. Don't let it slip away."

John shook his head. "Did we fail you on some level?"

He shook his head. "You've failed at nothing. Just... just please, hear this. Go with him to Switzerland. Be what I always wanted the two of you to be. You're brothers. I know you can do it together."

John leaned forward. With a shocked expression, he asked, "Do what together?"

His grandfather opened and shut his eyes. "Just do me the honor of going. I arranged the details, for the two of you. I should have talked to both of you years ago. You will find each other, I promise." He shook his head and appeared to be in pain. "A lot of men died to get it, John, a lot. Do that for me, won't you, son?" His head turned upwards to stare at the ceiling. His grip on the handrail loosened.

The rhythm of the heart monitor slowed while John waited to continue his conversation.

***

Later that morning at 11:05 A.M., Everett Devenger father of one deceased child and grandfather to three, passed from this life to the next.

Trumpicana

Acknowledgements

This was a twinkle in Kendall's eye. Ever the entrepreneur, he recognized an opportunity to use our creativity in an important way and maybe get notorious in the process.

He challenged me to write a satirical piece commenting on the current Presidential election process and all of its foibles, and dagnabbit, I did. And it came out pretty well. As did Kendall's. Together, we've made a political statement, and I am proud to be a part of it.

So my first acknowledgment is to him, for having the drive, the ideation and the energy to shove ideas into reality. Thanks, man. Once again, you rock.

But this was more than a two man effort.

A thousand thanks to Jessica Jaffe, who graced the cover of "The Day and The Hour" so well, that we hired her again. We once again owe her thanks for doing a fantabulous job of designing the cover of "Trumpicana". She is wonderful to work with and really tries to understand the goals and the message of the words between the covers, and then designs an awesome cover to match those aspirations. Well done, Jessica.

And a thousand more to Jason Seiler, world renowned caricaturist and illustrator, whose work has graced the covers of Rolling Stone, The New Yorker, Time magazine, and many other veritable news and entertainment media vehicles, who gave us an inspired rendition of the Orange Trump. We pitched him a crazy meme and he turned around and made it real. And it sings. It sweats. It scintillates. We are proud to have it as the mascot of our work. Thank you, Jason. You are a world class talent.

Lastly, and perversely, we have the pied piper madness of the current election cycle to thank: the venal media, the uncurated Internet, the dysfunctional politics, the loss of focus of what it means to be an American. Without all of this, the stories you hold in your hands today would not have been possible.

Kendall and I wish we didn't have to thank you for that. But thanks, anyway.

ABOUT THE AUTHORS

PRESLEY E. ACUNA writes unconventional thrillers, based in reality, but which take unexpected turns into the realms of fantasy, magical realism, science fiction and horror. His aim is to engage the reader in an engrossing mystery or adventure, while simultaneously using the situation to explore the deeper meanings of the ideas behind the story. When he is not writing, he is working as a systems engineer on the dot com frontier. He is also a musician, and formerly a member of the Supertones. He is a born and raised New Yorker, currently living in Brooklyn, but also enjoys spending time at his cabin, deep in the woods of western Massachusetts, with his wife and the host of critters that always manage to find their way into the house.

Trumpicana

KENDALL SMITH lives in Bergen County, New Jersey with his wife and giant baby boy, Connor. He is employed in the ad tech business in New York City and makes time to write before going to work and during the commute itself. He is the author of two novels: Vault 21-12 (Percussion Publishing, 2015) and Double-Edged Justice (2007) and both are available on Amazon and Kindle. In his spare time he is a drummer in a local New York City cover band, plays acoustic guitar and is an avid traveler.

Trumpicana

Trumpicana